To

....

HAPPY EASTER

Love

....

THE EASTER BUNNY
is coming to
MY TOWN

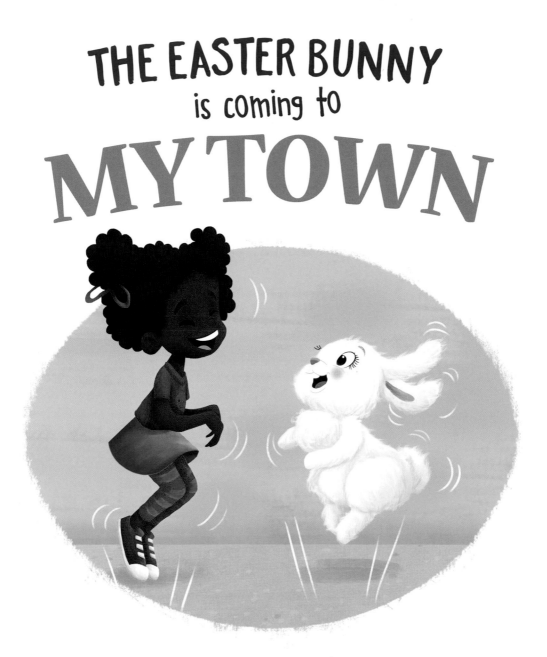

Written by Eric James Illustrated by Mari Lobo

sourcebooks
wonderland

The sweet Easter Bunny
is skipping along,
swinging her basket
and singing this song:

SUNNY DAY TOYS

OPEN

Easter
Parade
TODAY!

"The eggs are delivered.
My Easter job's done.
And now it is time
that I joined in the fun!"

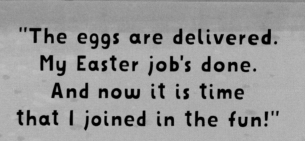

She jumps down a tunnel
that runs underground,
and pops up again
all around your home town.

In playgrounds, in parks,
and in backyards too.
I bet there's a tunnel
that's very near you!

She spots some young children
with paint on their faces,
and eggs decorated
like people and places!

SUNSHINE
PARK

But one little boy
drops the egg from his hands.
A loud CRACKING sound
can be heard as it lands.

"Oh dear!" says the bunny,
and dabs at a tear.
"You need cheering up
so thank goodness I'm here!"

She wiggles her ears,
she hops on the spot,
she waggles her tail,
and he giggles a lot!

She hops on till she sees
an Easter parade.
Most children are clapping
but one looks afraid.

HAPPY EASTER!

That clapping is noisy.
These legs are so TALL!
It's crowded and loud,
and she's ever so small!

"Gee whiz, what a din!
I know just what to do.
Come here little one
and I'll hold hands with you!"

She wiggles her ears,
and spins her around.
The little girl laughs
as her feet leave the ground!

Egg-rolling Race! →

A park bench is perfect
for having a rest.
She munches on lemon meringue pie.
(It's the best!)

Across in the park
there's an egg-rolling race.
A small boy falls down
and he's now lost his place!

The bunny trips up
as she's going to help.
She falls down the hill
with an **OUCH** and a YELP!

YELP!

OUCH!

She's just a big blur
as she tumbles on past.
The boy runs to help her.
He's going so FAST!

FINISH

She wiggles her ears,
he can't (but he tries!).
They hop up and down
for they've just won first prize!

This little girl's sad;
she's lost her stuffed bear.
Where could she have left him?
She's looked everywhere!

Roses
just in!

"When I'm feeling blue
do you know what I do?
I hop up and down!
Do you want to try too?"

She wiggles her ears, the girl thinks it's funny,
and laughs even more when she hops like a bunny!

They both jump around like they haven't a care.
And look what the chicks have just found, over there!

The bunny bounds on to help
children with SHARING.

And teaches a few to be
slightly more DARING.

LAKE

She **DANCES** and **SINGS**,
She **HOPS** and **WIGGLES**.

Wherever she goes,
she brings **LAUGHTER** and **GIGGLES**!

This day's been so busy
but also such fun.
The bunny daydreams
in the warm setting sun.

The twilight is coming,
the three chicks are lazing,
and tweeting about
how this day's been #AMAZING!

The bunny jumps up,
snapping out of her daze,
"There's only three-hundred-
and-sixty-four days!"

364
DAYS

More chocolate needs making!
New eggs will need wrapping!
It's all so exciting,
the three chicks start flapping!

"This town is so great and we love being here. We'll make lots more eggs and we'll be back next year!"

She wrinkles her nose,
she wiggles her ears,
she blows you a kiss,
and she just...disappears!

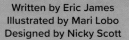

Written by Eric James
Illustrated by Mari Lobo
Designed by Nicky Scott

Published by Sourcebooks Wonderland,
an imprint of Sourcebooks Kids
P.O. Box 4410, Naperville, Illinois 60567-4410
(630) 961-3900
sourcebookskids.com

Date of Production: October 2021
Run Number: 5023516
Printed and bound in China (1010)
10 9 8 7 6 5 4 3